# A Note to Parents

Welcome to REAL KIDS READERS, a series of phonics-based books for children who are beginning to read. In the classroom, educators use phonics to teach children how to sound out unfamiliar words, providing a firm foundation for reading skills. At home, you can use REAL KIDS READERS to reinforce and build on that foundation, because the books follow the same basic phonic guidelines that children learn in school.

Of course the best way to help your child become a good reader is to make the experience fun—and REAL KIDS READERS do that, too. With their realistic story lines and lively characters, the books engage children's imaginations. With their clean design and sparkling photographs, they provide picture clues that help new readers decipher the text. The combination is sure to entertain young children and make them truly want to read.

REAL KIDS READERS have been developed at three distinct levels to make it easy for children to read at their own pace.

- LEVEL 1 is for children who are just beginning to read.
- LEVEL 2 is for children who can read with help.
- LEVEL 3 is for children who can read on their own.

A controlled vocabulary provides the framework at each level. Repetition, rhyme, and humor help increase word skills. Because children can understand the words and follow the stories, they quickly develop confidence. They go back to each book again and again, increasing their proficiency and sense of accomplishment, until they're ready to move on to the next level. The result is a rich and rewarding experience that will help them develop a lifelong love of reading.

*p B*

# Special thanks to Country Time Cycle, Mattituck, NY, for providing Sam's bicycle.

Produced by DWAI / Seventeenth Street Productions, Inc.

Real Kids Readers and the Real Kids Readers logo are trademarks of The Millbrook Press, Inc.

*Library of Congress Cataloging-in-Publication Data*

Ling, Bettina.
  Lemonade for Sale / by Bettina Ling ; photography by Dorothy Handelman.
      p.        cm. — (Real kids readers. Level 3)
  Summary: With the help of her friends, Kate overcomes several obstacles and sells enough lemonade in the neighborhood park to buy her father a birthday present.
  ISBN 0-7613-2010-5 (lib. bdg.). — ISBN 0-7613-2035-0 (pbk.)
  [1. Money-making projects—Fiction. 2. Lemonade—Fiction. 3. Birthdays—Fiction.] I. Handelman, Dorothy, ill. II. Title. III. Series.
PZ7.L66245Le  1998
[Fic]—dc21
                                                              97-31370
                                                              CIP
                                                              AC

pbk: 10 9 8 7 6 5 4 3 2 1
lib:  10 9 8 7 6 5 4 3 2 1

# Lemonade for Sale

## Bettina Ling

Photographs by **Dorothy Handelman**

**M**

**The Millbrook Press**

Brookfield, Connecticut

Kate shook her piggy bank hard. One last dime fell out. "How much does that make?" she asked her friend Lisa.

"Nine dollars in all," said Lisa.

"That's not enough," said Kate.

Kate's little brother, Sam, came into the room. "What's not enough?" he asked. He hopped onto the bed and started bouncing. "Wow! Look at all the money. What are you going to do with it?"

"I *was* going to buy Dad a toolbox for his birthday," said Kate. "But the one I want costs twenty dollars. I only have nine."

Sam stopped bouncing. He picked up a dime and handed it to Kate. "You could buy Dad two gum balls," he said. "The big ones only cost five cents each."

"Very funny," she said. "Go play in your own room, Sam." She gently pushed him out the door. Then she and Lisa put the coins back in the bank.

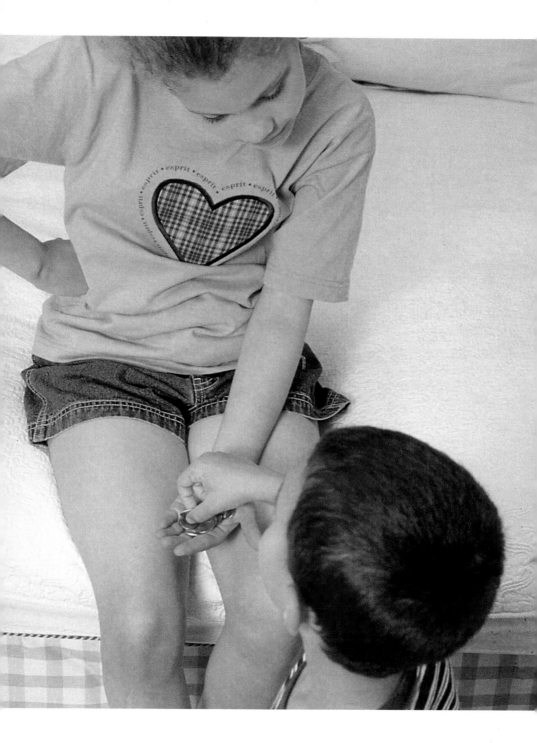

"Dad's birthday is only four days away," said Kate. "How am I going to get the rest of the money by then?"

"You'll think of a way," said Lisa. "In the meantime, let's go to the park. Nick and Max will be there by now."

The girls grabbed their baseball mitts. They walked through Kate's backyard gate into Pocket Park.

The park had houses on the sides and a gate at each end. It was small. But it was just the right size for Kate and her friends.

Max and Nick were playing catch.

"Hi, you guys," called Max. "Are you ready to play?" He threw the ball to Kate, but she missed the easy catch. Then, when she tossed the ball back, her throw went wild.

Max had to run after it.

The same thing happened the next time Kate threw the ball.

"Sorry, Max," she called as he ran after it. "I've got something on my mind."

"Like what?" Nick asked.

"Like how to get eleven dollars in three days," Kate said. "I need the money for my dad's birthday present."

Max came running back. He plopped onto a park bench. "Man, playing catch with you is hot work!" he said. "I wish I had a cold drink right now. I'd pour it down my throat like this. *Glug, glug, glug!*"

The other kids cracked up.

Then Kate thought of something. "That's it!" she yelled. "I know how to get the money. I'll sell lemonade, right here in Pocket Park."

"Good idea!" said Lisa. "Let's see. You'll need lemonade mix and cups and a stand."

"I'll get a table for the stand," said Max.

"I'll make some signs," said Nick.

"We'll all help!" said Lisa.

"Thanks, you guys," said Kate. "I bet I'll make lots of money."

"Enough to buy your dad *two* presents," said Nick. He gave Kate a high five.

Kate got the nine dollars from her bank. She went to the store with her mom. They bought lemonade mix and cups, and Kate still had money left over.

When she got home, Kate made two big jugs of lemonade. Lisa helped. Sam tasted.

"Just right," said Sam.

Nick and Max painted big signs. Some of them were a little messy, but Kate didn't mind.

Max got a folding table. He put it by one of the gates into Pocket Park. Lisa covered the table with a white cloth. Nick put up the signs. Kate put out the lemonade and cups. Then they all sat down to wait for their first sale.

They didn't have to wait long. A little girl came over from the swings.

"Oooh, lemonade! That looks good," she said. "I'll take a cup."

Kate poured the lemonade. "That will be fifty cents, please," she said with a grin.

The girl gave Kate the money. She sipped her lemonade. "Mmm. Yummy!" she said.

"Best lemonade in the park," said Nick.

"Best lemonade in the world!" said Max.

More people bought cups of lemonade. By the end of the day, Kate and her friends had made seven dollars.

Kate checked the jugs. "This is great," she said. "There's lots of lemonade left. And I still have two days to make the rest of the money."

"I'm sure you can do it," said Lisa.

Just then Sam rode into the park. "Hi, Kate!" he called. "Have you sold any lemonade yet?"

Kate grinned. "A whole bunch," she said.

Sam rode around the lemonade stand. "Watch this, you guys. No hands," he said. He let go of the handlebars.

"Look out!" Nick yelled.

"Stop, Sam!" Kate cried.

It was too late. Sam hit the table. *Crash!*
The jugs fell over. *Splash!* The lemonade
spilled all over the white cloth and onto the
ground.

"Sam!" Kate yelled. "Look what you did!"

"Not a smart move, Sammy," said Max.

Sam looked as if he were about to cry.
"I'm sorry. I didn't mean to do it," he said.

Kate rolled her eyes. "It's okay, Sam. I can buy more lemonade mix. I just hope I can still make my twenty dollars."

"I have an idea," said Nick. "Why don't you sell cookies too? Then you'll make more money."

"Good thinking," said Kate. "There's only one problem. I'd have to spend more money to buy stuff to make the cookies."

Kate told her mom what had happened.

"I'll make cookies for you," said her mom. She took Kate to the store to get more lemonade mix. Then she made a big batch of sugar cookies. This time Sam helped and Kate tasted.

"Just right," said Kate.

The next day, Kate and her friends made three dollars selling lemonade. They made two dollars selling sugar cookies.

"I've got more than half the money," said Kate. "I know I'll make the rest."

Kate set up her stand early the next day. Lisa came to help. "I bet you sell lots of lemonade today," she said. "The air feels so hot and sticky."

Kate looked at the sky. It had been blue when she'd first set up. Now there were dark clouds covering the sun.

"I sure hope it doesn't rain," she said.

Just then a big, fat raindrop hit Kate's head. Then another and another.

"Quick!" she cried. "Grab the cookies and the lemonade before they get wet."

But now the rain was pouring down. The cookies got mushy. The lemonade got watery. The paper cups and the sign got soggy. And the girls got soaked.

Kate's lemonade stand was a big mess!

Kate tried not to cry. "Tomorrow is Dad's birthday," she said. "There's no way I'll have the money for his present."

"Don't give up yet," said Lisa. "You can still sell stuff in the morning."

Kate sighed. "I don't know," she said.

"Come on," said Lisa. "Give it a try."

"Okay," said Kate. "I'll try one more time."

Kate bought more lemonade mix and cups. She made more lemonade, and her mom made more cookies.

Max and Nick made a new sign.

The next morning, Kate and her friends went back to Pocket Park. But the street was all blocked off and the gates were closed. A sign hung on the fence.

Nick read it out loud. "Park closed today. Tree trimming."

"No selling lemonade today," Kate said sadly.

"Hi, there," called a man in a yellow hard hat. "What are you kids doing?"

"We were going to sell lemonade in the park," said Kate. "But it's closed."

"That's right," said the man. "My crew is trimming the trees today."

"I bet that's hard work," said Lisa.

"I bet it's *hot* work," Kate added quickly. "Would you like to buy some lemonade?"

The man grinned. "Cold lemonade would taste good," he said. "I'll buy both jugs for my crew—and the cookies too."

Kate and her friends cheered.

Now Kate had twenty-four dollars in all!
She bought the red toolbox for her dad.
Then she bought a box of ice-cream bars to
share with her friends.

"Thanks, you guys. I couldn't have done it
without you," Kate said.

"You're pretty good at selling stuff, Kate," said Max. "What are you going to sell next?"

"Guess," she said.

"Ice cream!" the kids yelled.

Everyone wanted to help.

# Reading with Your Child

Even though your child is reading more independently now, it is vital that you continue to take part in this important learning experience.

- Try to read with your child at least twenty minutes each day, as part of your regular routine.
- Encourage your child to keep favorite books in one convenient, cozy spot, so you don't waste valuable reading time looking for them.
- Read and familiarize yourself with the Phonic Guidelines on the next pages.
- Praise your young reader. Be the cheerleader, not the teacher. Your enthusiasm and encouragement are key ingredients in your child's success.

## What to Do if Your Child Gets Stuck on a Word

- Wait a moment to see if he or she works it out alone.
- Help him or her decode the word phonetically. Say, "Try to sound it out."
- Encourage him or her to use picture clues. Say, "What does the picture show?"
- Encourage him or her to use context clues. Say, "What would make sense?"
- Ask him or her to try again. Say, "Read the sentence again and start the tricky word. Get your mouth ready to say it."
- If your child still doesn't "get" the word, tell him or her what it is. Don't wait for frustration to build.

## What to Do if Your Child Makes a Mistake

- If the mistake makes sense, ignore it—unless it is part of a pattern of errors you wish to correct.
- If the mistake doesn't make sense, wait a moment to see if your child corrects it.
- If your child doesn't correct the mistake, ask him or her to try again, either by decoding the word or by using context or picture clues. Say, "Get your mouth ready" or "Make it sound right" or "Make it make sense."
- If your child still doesn't "get" the word, tell him or her what it is. Don't wait for frustration to build.

# Phonic Guidelines

Use the following guidelines to help your child read the words in this story.

## Short Vowels

When two consonants surround a vowel, the sound of the vowel is usually short. This means you pronounce *a* as in apple, *e* as in egg, *i* as in igloo, *o* as in octopus, and *u* as in umbrella. Words with short vowels include: *bed, big, box, cat, cup, dad, dog, get, hid, hop, hum, jam, kid, mad, met, mom, pen, ran, sad, sit, sun, top.*

## R-Controlled Vowels

When a vowel is followed by the letter *r*, its sound is changed by the *r*. Words with *r*-controlled vowels include: *card, curl, dirt, farm, girl, herd, horn, jerk, torn, turn.*

## Long Vowel and Silent E

If a word has a vowel followed by a consonant and an *e*, usually the vowel is long and the *e* is silent. Long vowels are pronounced the same way as their alphabet names. Words with a long vowel and silent *e* include: *bake, cute, dive, game, home, kite, mule, page, pole, ride, vote.*

## Double Vowels

When two vowels are side by side, usually the first vowel is long and the second vowel is silent. Words with double vowels include: *boat, clean, gray, loaf, meet, neat, paint, pie, play, rain, sleep, tried.*

## Diphthongs

Sometimes when two vowels (or a vowel and a consonant) are side by side, they combine to make a diphthong—a sound that is different from long or short vowel sounds. Diphthongs are: *au/aw, ew, oi/oy, ou/ow*. Words with diphthongs include: *auto, brown, claw, flew, found, join, toy.*

## Double Consonants

When two identical consonants appear side by side, one of them is silent. Words with double consonants include: *bell, fuss, mess, mitt, puff, tall, yell.*

## Consonant Blends

When two or more different consonants are side by side, they usually blend to make a combined sound. Words with consonant blends include: *bent, blob, bride, club, crib, drop, flip, frog, gift, glare, grip, help, jump, mask, most, pink, plane, ring, send, skate, sled, spin, steep, swim, trap, twin.*

## Consonant Digraphs
Sometimes when two different consonants are side by side, they make a digraph that represents a single new sound. Consonant digraphs are: *ch, sh, th, wh*. Words with digraphs include: *bath, chest, lunch, sheet, think, whip, wish*.

## Silent Consonants
Sometimes when two different consonants are side by side, one of them is silent. Words with silent consonants include: *back, dumb, knit, knot, lamb, sock, walk, wrap, wreck*.

## Sight Words
Sight words are those words that a reader must learn to recognize immediately—by sight—instead of by sounding them out. They occur with high frequency in easy texts. Sight words include: *a, am, an, and, as, at, be, big, but, can, come, do, for, get, give, have, he, her, his, I, in, is, it, just, like, look, make, my, new, no, not, now, old, one, out, play, put, red, run, said, see, she, so, some, soon, that, the, then, there, they, to, too, two, under, up, us, very, want, was, we, went, what, when, where, with, you*.

## Exceptions to the "Rules"
Although much of the English language is phonically regular, there are many words that don't follow the above guidelines. For example, a particular combination of letters can represent more than one sound. Double *oo* can represent a long *oo* sound, as in words such as *boot, cool,* and *moon*; or it can represent a short *oo* sound, as in words such as *foot, good,* and *hook*. The letters *ow* can represent a diphthong, as in words such as *brow, fowl,* and *town*; or they can represent a long *o* sound, as in words such as *blow, snow,* and *tow*. Additionally, some high-frequency words such as *some, come, have,* and *said* do not follow the guidelines at all, and *ough* appears in such different-sounding words as *although, enough,* and *thought*.

The phonic guidelines provided in this book are just that—guidelines. They do not cover all the irregularities in our rich and varied language, but are intended to correspond roughly to the phonic lessons taught in the the first and second grades. Phonics provides the foundation for learning to read. Repetition, visual clues, context, and sheer experience provide the rest.